Out to Lunch

For The Breakfast Club:
Rena, Patrice, Marcy, and Vivian
—N.K.

ISBN 0-439-77482-9

12 11 10 9   9 10/0

Printed in the U.S.A.   40

First Scholastic printing, May 2005

Out to Lunch

by Nancy Krulik
illustrated by John & Wendy

SCHOLASTIC INC.

New York Toronto London Auckland Sydney
Mexico City New Delhi Hong Kong Buenos Aires

Chapter 1

"How many tomatoes are you going to eat?" Katie Carew asked her friend Kevin Camilleri as she plopped down into the seat across from him in the school cafeteria. Kevin had opened his lunch box. Inside were all sorts of tomatoes—tiny grape tomatoes; small, round cherry tomatoes; oval-shaped plum tomatoes; and a big plastic bag filled with sliced tomatoes. And for dessert, he had a bag of tomato-flavored chips.

Kevin picked up one of the oval-shaped tomatoes and bit into it like an apple. "I could probably eat about a million of these. I love tomatoes!"

All the kids at the table laughed. They knew that Kevin had been a tomato freak since kindergarten. Back then they had even nicknamed him Tomato Man.

"You've never met a tomato you didn't like, right, Kevin?" Katie teased.

"That's not true," Kevin said. "I'd never eat a tomato from the school salad bar."

The kids at the table agreed. The vegetables at the salad bar were pretty gross.

"Hey, how do you stop a rotten tomato from smelling?" George Brennan asked, dropping his tray down next to Katie. George loved jokes and riddles. He told them all the time.

"How?" Kevin asked him.

"Hold its nose!" George answered. He began laughing hysterically. He turned to Katie. "Good one, huh, Katie Kazoo?"

Katie giggled. She loved George's jokes. She didn't even mind when he called her Katie Kazoo. She thought the nickname sounded sort of cool! She'd even tried signing

Katie Kazoo on her schoolwork—until her teacher, Mrs. Derkman, made her write her real name on her papers.

"Whoops," Katie knocked her spoon off the table when she laughed. "Hold my place George," she told him. "I'll be right back."

Katie got up from the table and walked over to the lunch counter. "May I have a spoon?" she asked the lunch lady.

"Didn't you get one already?" the lunch lady answered in a very grouchy voice.

"I dropped it," Katie explained.

"Tough toenails," the lunch lady told her. "One spoon per customer."

"But how am I going to eat my pudding?"

The lunch lady rolled her eyes. "Use your hands. Or better yet, don't eat it at all. I wouldn't."

The lunch lady hadn't been very nice. But she was probably right. The pudding looked disgusting, and it smelled worse. Katie *was* better off not eating it.

Katie went back to the lunch table. She sat down and looked at her apple. If she ate around the rotten spot, it might be okay.

"Got room over here for me?" Suzanne Lock asked.

Katie scooted over to make room for her best friend. Suzanne put down her cafeteria tray and sat beside Katie.

"I thought you were sitting at the other

table with Jeremy," Katie said. She looked over at the long table in the corner, where Jeremy Fox sat with two boys from the other third grade class. Katie had known Jeremy and Suzanne practically since they were babies. Jeremy and Suzanne were pals, but they didn't think of each other as best friends. Katie considered both of them her best friends, though.

"Jeremy's looking at some dumb baseball book," Suzanne explained. "It's soooo boring!" She placed her spoon into her bowl of  alphabet soup and fished around. A moment later, she lifted the spoon and smiled. "Look! I spelled rat!"

Katie looked onto Suzanne's spoon. Sure enough, the letters R, A, and T were sitting in a sea of light orange water.

Katie giggled.

Suzanne put the spoon in her mouth and

made a funny face. "Even a rat wouldn't eat this stuff," she said. "It's terrible—just water with food coloring! It has no flavor at all."

Katie nodded. "I know what you mean. The food in this cafeteria is awful, and almost everything is made with some sort of meat. All I ever get to eat for lunch is a stale bagel and Jell-O."

"Oh, come on, Katie. Sometimes they serve gloppy, overcooked macaroni and cheese and old carrot sticks," Suzanne teased. "You can eat that."

"Yuck!" Katie exclaimed.

"That's what you get for being a vegetarian." Kevin told Katie.

"Did you hear the one about the guy with carrot sticks stuck in his ears?" George interrupted.

Katie shook her head. "No."

"That's okay," George shrugged. "He didn't hear it either!"

As George laughed at his own joke,

Suzanne frowned. "That one was really bad, George," she said. She turned back to Katie. "The fried chicken nuggets aren't too bad, and they serve those a lot. I don't know why you won't even eat a piece of chicken once in a while."

"I told you, I won't eat anything that had a face," Katie explained.

"But chickens have *ugly* faces," Kevin pointed out.

"I won't eat any animals," Katie insisted. "Of course, that doesn't leave me with many choices in the cafeteria."

"Why don't you ask your mom to pack your lunches?" Miriam Chan suggested as she took a bite of a turkey sandwich her mother had packed.

"She doesn't have time," Katie explained. "On the days she opens the store, she leaves for work at the same time I leave for school. Our house is crazy in the mornings." Katie's mom worked part time at The Book Nook, a small bookstore in the Cherrydale Mall.

"Well, I'm glad my mom packs my lunch," Kevin said. "That way, I don't ever have to face the *Lunch Lady*!" He made a scary face.

"You know what happened to me today?" Suzanne said. "I asked the lunch lady if I could have a banana that wasn't totally brown and mushy. You know what she told me? She said, 'If you want fresh fruit, get it from home. Brown mushy bananas are what's on the cafeteria menu today.' "

"She's such a grump!" Kevin said.

"You'd be grumpy too if you had to dish out smelly, disgusting food all day," Katie told him.

"That's true," Suzanne agreed.

"Speaking of disgusting, look at George!" Zoe Canter exclaimed. "I think I'm gonna throw up!"

Katie looked over at George's tray. It was totally gross. George had mixed his mashed potatoes and vegetable soup together. Then he'd poured his chocolate milk into the mix. Now he was busy stirring in some orange Jell-O.

"Hey, Katie Kazoo, do you dare me to eat this?" he asked her.

Katie made a face. "Yuck!" she exclaimed.

Suzanne stood and picked up her tray. "Come on, Katie," she said. "Let's get out of here before George really does eat that mess."

As Katie and Suzanne headed toward the playground for recess, Suzanne looked back at George and sighed. "Boys can be so dumb," she remarked.

Katie shrugged. Some boys could be pretty

dumb. But other boys were really cool. Like Jeremy. Katie was about to say that, but she stopped herself. Suzanne got mad whenever Katie talked about Jeremy. Suzanne didn't like to think that Katie had two best friends.

"Come on, hurry up!" Suzanne urged Katie. "Let's see if we can get to the hop-scotch game before the fourth-graders do!"

Katie followed her friend out the door.

Katie tossed her stone toward the hop-scotch board. It landed in the middle of the three. Quickly Katie began jumping up and down the board. As she bent down to pick up her stone on the way back, she heard Jeremy's voice over her head.

"You guys want to throw the ball around a little bit?" he asked.

Katie hopped off the board and smiled at Jeremy. "Maybe later," she said. "We're kind of in the middle of a game."

Suzanne gave a deep sigh. "He can see

that, Katie." She turned to Jeremy. "Can't you?"

Jeremy nodded. "I just thought maybe you two would want to play catch, that's all. You said you wanted to work on your aim," he reminded Katie.

"I do," Katie said kindly. "How about after we finish with hopscotch?"

Jeremy shrugged and pushed his glasses further up on his nose. "Sure. See ya later."

As Jeremy walked off, Katie looked at Suzanne. "You sounded kind of angry. Are you mad at Jeremy or something?" she asked.

Suzanne shook her head. "No. I just thought it was really rude of him to try to break up our game."

Katie nodded. "I guess we could have asked him if he wanted to play with us instead."

"He wouldn't have wanted to play hop-scotch," Suzanne told Katie. "None of the boys play hopscotch anymore."

Katie shrugged. Suzanne was probably

right. But they could have asked Jeremy to play anyway, just to be nice.

Just then Mandy Banks came strolling over. Miriam and Zoe were right behind her. They were each carrying flat, smooth stones—perfect for hopscotch.

"Can we play with you?" Mandy asked.

Suzanne smiled brightly. "Sure. You're right after Katie, Mandy. Then Zoe, then Miriam. This game is for third-grade girls only . . . right Katie?"

Katie didn't answer. She didn't like it when games were just for girls or just for boys. She was much happier when everybody got to play. Katie tucked her red hair behind her ears. Then she reached out and tossed her stone toward the square with the four in it. The small rock soared right over the box, and landed on the eight instead.

"Your turn, Mandy," Suzanne called out cheerfully.

Chapter 2

Classroom 3A was a wild place after lunch.

"Look out, incoming plane," George shouted as he threw a paper airplane toward Kevin.

Kevin laughed. "Back at ya!" He tossed the plane back to George.

Suzanne ducked as the paper plane shot over her head. "Hey! Watch it!" she shouted at Kevin.

"That's enough now," Mrs. Derkman told the class. "Recess is over. Please take out your writer's notebooks. We're going to work on our biographies."

Katie smiled. She loved writing biographies. Right now she was working on one about her dog, Pepper. Katie had taken care of him since he was a puppy. Pepper was like a brother to her—even better because Pepper didn't argue or ask to share her toys.

Squeak. Squeak. Squeak. Katie looked over toward the class hamster's cage. Boy, did Speedy's wheel need oiling.

Mrs. Derkman must have heard the squeaking, too, because she said, "Oh, class, before I forget—the classroom floors are being cleaned this weekend. I will need someone to take Speedy home. If you're interested, bring me a note from your parents saying it's okay."

Katie knew she couldn't even think about bringing Speedy home for the weekend—not with Pepper living there. Dogs and hamsters didn't always get along so well.

Still, Katie really wished she could take Speedy home. She cared about him more than anyone else in the whole class. Maybe that was because Katie was the only one in the class who had actually been Speedy.

It was true! Katie had actually turned into the class hamster for a whole morning!

It happened a few weeks ago. After a really, really bad day, Katie had made the mistake of wishing she could be anyone but herself.

There must have been some sort of shooting star flying through the sky at the very moment Katie had made the wish, because it had come true. (And everyone knows when you make a wish on a shooting star, it comes true!) The only thing was, instead of turning into some*one* else, Katie had turned into some*thing* else—Speedy!

Katie shivered a little as she remembered being a hamster. It was really scary. She thought she'd be stuck in that tiny, smelly glass cage forever. But eventually she'd gotten loose. And luckily, once she was free, Katie had somehow turned back into herself.

Katie didn't understand how any of it had happened. All she knew was that she was really glad to be an eight-year-old girl again.

Ever since she'd spent time in Speedy's body, Katie had taken great care of the little hamster. She always made sure his water bowl was full, gave him plenty of chew sticks, and brought him fresh carrots from home.

Of course, Katie had never told anyone about turning into Speedy. She didn't think they would believe her. She wouldn't have believed it if it hadn't happened to her.

"Hey, Katie Kazoo, if I took Speedy home, you know what I would do with him?" George whispered from the desk next to Katie's.

"What?" Katie whispered back.

"Keep him in the refrigerator," George answered.

Katie looked at George with surprise. "Why would you do that?"

"To keep him from getting spoiled," George told her. "Nobody likes a spoiled hamster!"

Katie smiled and sighed. She knew George was only joking. George would never take Speedy home. He was afraid of hamsters!

As soon as the school bell rang, Katie packed up her backpack and hurried toward the door. She couldn't wait to get out of the school. It had been a very long afternoon.

Jeremy and Katie met up on the school's front steps. "I'm definitely asking my mother if I can take Speedy home," he announced.

Katie smiled. She knew how badly Jeremy wanted a pet. His mother kept saying she was waiting to see if he was responsible enough to care for one. "Great!" Katie exclaimed. "Once your mom sees how you feed Speedy, give him water, and change the dirty litter in his cage, she'll get you your own pet for sure."

"I have to change the litter?" Jeremy asked, scrunching up his nose.

"Of course," Katie told him. "Otherwise, it starts to stink!"

Before Jeremy could answer, Suzanne

came bounding down the steps toward them. "I'm so excited!" she announced.

"How come?" Katie asked her.

" 'Cause I'm going to ask my mom to let me bring Speedy home this weekend. It'll be so much fun to have him there. I'm going to build him a whole hamster playground. I can use toilet paper tubes, egg cartons, and . . . "

"Wait a minute," Jeremy interrupted her. "*You're* not bringing Speedy home."

"Why not?" Suzanne asked.

"Because *I'm* bringing him home," he told her.

"Are not!" Suzanne exclaimed.

"Am, too!" Jeremy shouted back.

"Yeah, who says?" Suzanne demanded.

"I do!" Jeremy yelled.

Suzanne looked straight at Katie. "Which one of us do *you* think Speedy should go home with?" she asked.

Katie wasn't sure what to say. As she looked from Jeremy to Suzanne, she wasn't

sure who Speedy would be happier with.
Jeremy promised he would take good care of
Speedy, but Katie knew Jeremy had a Little
League game on Saturday. What if he was so
busy thinking about baseball that he forgot to
feed Speedy?

On the other hand, Suzanne might not be

able to take care of Speedy very well, either. Suzanne's mom had just had a new baby. Now that little Heather had arrived, things were really crazy at Suzanne's house. People were always stopping by to see the new baby, and everyone was busy running around, changing diapers and heating up bottles. What if someone knocked the lid off of Speedy's cage by accident? The hamster would be long gone before anyone in her house even realized he'd escaped.

"Come on, Katie, who do you think should get to take Speedy home?" Suzanne asked Katie again.

Katie had a sick feeling in her stomach. No matter what she said, somebody would be mad at her. So, instead of making a decision, Katie walked away. "I have to get home and feed Pepper," she told her friends quickly. "Talk to you later."

Chapter 3

The next day there was trouble in room 3A.
Jeremy and Suzanne both came to school
with notes from their parents saying they
could bring Speedy home for the weekend.
Katie hoped that Mrs. Derkman would just
pick one kid or the other to take the hamster.
But that's not what the teacher decided to do.

"You two will have to work this out
between you," Mrs. Derkman told Jeremy and
Suzanne. "You have until the end of the week
to tell me what you decide."

Katie thought that was just about the most
terrible thing her teacher could have done.
Neither Jeremy nor Suzanne was going to

give in. It didn't seem like her friends even cared about taking care of Speedy anymore. All they cared about was winning.

The whole class was caught up in the war between Suzanne and Jeremy. All the boys were siding with Jeremy. The girls were all on Suzanne's side—except Katie. She didn't know whose side to be on. Jeremy and Suzanne were both her best friends.

Unfortunately, Jeremy and Suzanne weren't friends with each other anymore.

"You're going to sit with me, aren't you, Katie?" Suzanne asked as class 3A walked into the cafeteria.

"Who says she's gonna sit with you?" Jeremy interrupted. "She was my friend before she ever met you."

Suzanne rolled her eyes. "That's just because your moms knew each other when they were kids," she explained. "You guys probably wouldn't have become friends if it weren't for that."

George pulled a bag of potato chips from his lunch bag. "Do you know why best friends are like potatoes?" he asked jokingly.

"No, why?" Katie said.

"Because they're always there when the *chips* are down!" George started to laugh. "Get it?"

Katie smiled. She was glad George was trying to make everyone laugh. "That was funny," she told him.

Suzanne put her arm around Katie. "Katie's like that," she told the others. "She's always on *my* side."

Jeremy moved closer toward Katie. "No, she's always on my side," he argued.

Katie could feel the tears starting to build

 up in her eyes. This just wasn't fair. "Look, you guys, I like both of you. I don't want to have to choose. I wish I could just cut myself in half," she said.

George started to laugh.

"What's so funny about that?" Katie demanded.

"Nothing." George shrugged. "It's just that I was thinking, if you cut your left side off, you'd be *all right*." He laughed again.

But for once Katie didn't laugh with him. She felt like nothing was going to be alright ever again. Quickly she turned and ran back into the hall. "I have to go to the bathroom," she mumbled as she darted away.

Katie walked into the girls' room and looked around. There was no one else there. It was nice to be alone. Maybe she could just stay in the bathroom until lunch was over. That way she could keep away from Suzanne, Jeremy, and everyone else in her class.

Katie looked at her watch. It was 12:05. Lunch was over at 1:00. That meant she would have to stay in the girls' room for fifty-five minutes. That was a very long time. What could she do in the bathroom for fifty-five minutes? Katie looked at her watch again. Make that fifty-four minutes. The hands on her watch had just moved to 12:06.

Well, for starters, she could wash her face and hands. Katie turned on the water and held her hands under the faucet.

Suddenly Katie felt a light wind blowing on her back. She looked up toward the bathroom window. It was closed. So was the door. The wind wasn't coming from outside. It was only blowing in the girls' room. Katie gulped as she looked around her. The wind didn't even seem to be blowing anywhere else in the room—just around Katie.

The wind grew stronger and stronger, swirling around her like a tornado. For a minute Katie was sure it was going to lift her right off the ground—like Dorothy in *The Wizard of Oz*. She closed her eyes and grabbed on to the sink, trying to keep herself from flying away.

Katie was really scared. She knew what

trouble this kind of wind could cause. This
wasn't the first time Katie had been trapped
in a strange, magical windstorm. It had happened to her twice before, once when she'd
turned into Speedy, and once when she'd

turned back into herself. This wind could only mean one thing.

Katie Carew was becoming somebody else!

But who?

Or *what*?

After a few seconds, the wind stopped. Everything was quiet—and different. There was a really bad stink in the air. Not a bathroom stink, though. It smelled more like spoiled milk.

"Ow!" Katie yanked her hand from the sink. The cool plaster had suddenly turned really hot.

Where was she?

She slowly opened her eyes and looked nervously toward the mirror. It was time to find out just who she'd changed into.

But as Katie's eyelids fluttered open, she discovered there was no mirror in front of her. There was no sink, either. Katie wasn't even in the bathroom. She was in the cafeteria! She'd just burned her hand on the hot lunch counter.

A really bad smell began to waft up from the table.

"Yuck! What stinks?" Katie said aloud.

She looked down at a stack of disgusting gray hamburgers. Beside the burgers was a pile of old slices of American cheese. One of the slices was covered in green mold. Spoiled cheese and bad hamburgers—Katie felt sick.

Beads of sweat began to form on her forehead. Katie raised her hand to wipe them away. That's when she saw that her hands were much larger than usual—the size of adult hands. She was also wearing clear plastic gloves that made her big hands feel hot and sweaty.

Katie ran her gloved hands over her dress. The dress was mostly white, but there were brown gravy stains all over it. Some of the stains looked like they'd been there for a while. Others looked as though they'd just landed on the dress today.

As Katie reached up to wipe a bead of

sweat from her cheek, she felt a sharp pain in her lower back—the kind her mother complained about when she'd spent too many hours standing up at work. Katie's feet really hurt, too. As she looked down, she was amazed to see just how huge her feet had become. Her white shoes looked like big boats on the ends of her legs!

"Excuse me," a fourth-grade boy said to Katie. "Can I have a hot dog and a carton of milk?"

That's when Katie realized what had happened to her.

Katie Carew had turned into Lucille the lunch lady!

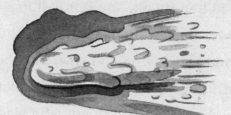

Chapter 4

Now what? Katie thought nervously. *I can't do this. I don't want to touch that disgusting meat.*

"What's going on up there?" a sixth-grade girl shouted from the back of the line.

"The lunch lady is so slow," someone else said.

Katie felt like crying. She wasn't used to having kids yell at her. She didn't think being Lucille would be very much fun, but there was nothing she could do about it now.

Katie's only hope was that she had only been stuck inside Speedy's body for a little while. Maybe that's how it would work with

Lucille's body, too. Maybe the magic wind would change Katie back into herself pretty soon. She sure hoped so.

"Come on! Move it!" a sixth-grader shouted.

The kids were getting really mad. Katie wished she could just run away and hide, but there was nowhere for her to go. Katie had no choice. She was Lucille. She had to do what Lucille would do.

She had to serve disgusting food to kids.

"Oh man, not hot dogs again," a fifth-grade boy named Carlos moaned as he stared at a bucket of hot dogs swimming around in boiling water. "We had those yesterday, and three days before that."

"I know how you feel," Katie agreed. "I'm pretty sick of these hounds with Mississippi mud myself. Would you rather have a wimpy instead?"

Hounds with Mississippi mud? Wimpy? Katie was shocked as the weird words left her mouth. She'd never even heard those words before. But somehow she just seemed to know that a hound with Mississippi mud was a hot dog with mustard, and that a wimpy was a hamburger.

It must be some sort of lunchroom code that only lunch ladies know, Katie thought to herself.

"Who are you calling wimpy?" Carlos demanded in an angry voice.

Katie blushed. "Nobody. Wimpy means hamburger."

"Huh?" Carlos asked her.

"Oh, never mind." Katie replied in her best lunch lady voice. "Just move along."

A sixth-grade boy named Malcolm was next in line. "What's the sandwich today?" he asked her.

"Hen fruit," Katie answered. Oops! There was that lunchroom lingo again. "Uh, I mean egg salad," she explained quickly.

"Blech!" Malcolm exclaimed. "I hate egg salad."

Katie sighed. These kids were so mean. They were acting as though she'd cooked the food or something. She knew she had nothing to do with this menu. Lunch ladies weren't chefs. They just served what they were given. It wasn't like she was having a whole lot of fun serving the stuff, either. It was awful standing back there behind the counter, having to stare at rotting fruit and sniffing the scent of boiled hot dogs, overcooked baked beans, and egg salad all day long.

But Katie couldn't argue with Malcolm. She only had to *serve* the food. He actually had to eat it. Katie smiled at him and nodded her head. "I don't like egg salad very much, either," she said as she pointed to the egg salad tray. "Especially *this* egg salad. It's all gloppy. Too much mayonnaise."

"Like always," Malcolm moaned.

"You know where this egg salad belongs?" she asked Malcolm as she picked up a huge scooper full of the yellow-white glop.

"Where?" Malcolm said.

Katie gave him a naughty smile. "In the garbage!" she announced. Then she hurled the egg salad toward the garbage can.

Malcolm stared at her with surprise. He'd never seen Lucille the lunch lady throw food in the garbage before. Nobody had.

Katie watched as the big ball of egg salad soared in the direction of the trash can. Unfortunately, Katie's aim was not very good. The egg salad landed right on top of George's tray.

Katie gulped. *Maybe I should've worked on my throwing with Jeremy yesterday,* she thought to herself. Katie looked nervously at George. She couldn't tell if he was angry or not.

A big smile flashed across George's face. "*Food fight!*" he announced loudly. George shot a big glob of strawberry yogurt right at Kevin. The yogurt landed on a pile of tomato slices inside Kevin's lunch box.

Katie gasped. George shouldn't have done that. He knew how Kevin felt about tomatoes. Kevin was going to be really mad that George had ruined some of them!

A fifth-grader named Stanley was sitting at the next table. He began to laugh. "Looks like your lunch is gone," Stanley told Kevin. "You can't eat it now."

Kevin nodded. "I know. But there are lots of things you can do with a tomato!" He picked up a yogurt-covered tomato slice and flung it right at Stanley. The round slice landed in the middle of the fifth-grader's shirt. "Bulls-eye!" Kevin called out excitedly.

After that, it seemed like everyone in the entire cafeteria started throwing food. Stanley tossed his jelly sandwich toward the table where class 3A was sitting. It landed right on Jeremy's face. Suzanne began to giggle as Jeremy wiped grape jelly from his glasses. Jeremy threw a glob of mashed potatoes at Suzanne. Suzanne rolled a piece of hot dog bun into a little ball and threw it at Jeremy.

Mandy was so busy watching Suzanne and Jeremy that she didn't notice a hot dog with mustard flying towards her. It landed right on her head. "Oooh! Gross!" she shouted out. The hot dog slid onto the floor below, but the mustard stayed in Mandy's hair.

Miriam started giggling. Mandy grinned and shook her head wildly—splashing yellow mustard all over Miriam.

Miriam picked up a slice of salami and threw it at Mandy. Mandy ducked. The salami landed on Zoe's nose.

George laughed so hard he fell off his

chair and landed on the floor. Zoe picked up her milk and poured it over George's head. George wiped the milk from his eyes, smiled, and licked his lips. "Mmmm!" he exclaimed. "Chocolate. My favorite!"

The kids were going wild! They launched lunchmeat. They flung frankfurters. They heaved hamburgers. Everyone and everything was covered with food. The teachers tried to stop the food fight, but they couldn't. The lunchroom was a mess.

Katie looked up. A canned peach was flying straight at her head. She ducked. The bright orange fruit smacked into the wall behind her and slid toward the floor.

"Look out!" Katie cried as she scooped up two huge handfuls of green Jell-O. "Here comes a Jell-O bomb!" She reached back and threw the glop across the room. The slimy Jell-O flew through the air and landed with a splat . . . *right in the middle of Mr. Kane's forehead*.

Katie had just slimed the school principal!

"Lucille!" Mr. Kane shouted in a very angry voice as he wiped the gooey green stuff from his eyes. "I'll see you in my office in fifteen minutes!"

The entire lunchroom froze. All eyes were on Katie.

Oh no! Katie had totally forgotten she was the lunch lady. She was in big trouble now. "Yes, sir," Katie told the principal, in Lucille's low, grown-up voice.

"As for you students," Mr. Kane continued, "you will be spending the rest of your day cleaning this cafeteria."

Chapter 5

As Katie walked down the hall, she felt a little sick. She had never been called down to the principal's office before—ever. Katie had never done anything bad in school in her whole life. *Until now.*

Katie knew Mr. Kane was going to give her a terrible punishment. She guessed it wasn't going to be something easy, like having to stay after school or writing a long apology note. This was going to be some sort of *grown-up* punishment. After all, Mr. Kane thought he was punishing Lucille the lunch lady, not Katie Carew from class 3A.

Suddenly Katie felt a gentle wind nip at

the back of her neck. She looked behind to see if someone had just opened a door or a window. No one was there.

Katie wasn't surprised when the calm wind began to get stronger. She wasn't shocked when it started blowing wildly around her like a tornado, either. She knew what was about to happen. Katie was going to change into someone else.

"Please, please, please let me turn back into me," she cried to the wind. "I just want to be Katie Carew. Nobody else."

The wind kept blowing harder and harder. Katie closed her eyes and held on tight to one of the lockers.

After a few minutes, the tornado stopped. The wind just disappeared, leaving no marks or traces in the hall. Not even one piece of paper was out of place. Slowly, Katie opened her eyes and looked down. Lucille's gravy-stained white dress was gone. Black jeans and a white sweater had taken its place. Those were the clothes Katie had worn to school that morning. Katie checked her reflection in a nearby classroom window. An eight-year-old girl with red hair, green eyes, and a line of

freckles on her nose looked back at her from the glass.

Katie Carew was back!

As Katie smiled at her reflection, she heard Mr. Kane's voice coming from his office.

"Lucille! I don't know what's gotten into you!" the principal yelled.

"I don't know what's gotten into me, either, Mr. Kane," Lucille said. "Come to think of it, I don't even know how I wound up here in your office."

Katie was surprised to hear the lunch lady's voice. How had she gotten to Mr. Kane's office so quickly? Did she know what had happened in the cafeteria? Did she remember that Katie had been inside her body?

"One minute, I'm in the cafeteria, handing out food. The next minute I'm standing here," Lucille continued. "I can't really remember anything in between."

"*Handing out food?*" Mr. Kane demanded. "Is that what you call slinging Jell-O across the cafeteria?"

"No sir," Lucille answered.

"Are you saying you *didn't* throw food in the cafeteria?" Mr. Kane asked her.

"No. I think I did throw food."

"You *think* you threw food?" Mr. Kane repeated.

Lucille shrugged. "I'm pretty sure I did . . . I think. I don't know. You saw me throw it, right?"

Mr. Kane nodded.

"So I must have," Lucille continued. "It's all very strange. I guess I just wasn't myself today."

"I can't understand what would make you waste perfectly good food," Mr. Kane continued.

"Well, I wouldn't call it 'perfectly good food,' " Lucille argued. "It's terrible food. We need to give those kids fresh fruits and vegetables, and there need to be more choices on the menu. I can understand why the kids treated the food like garbage. It *is* garbage. Now if I were in charge . . . "

That made Mr. Kane more angry than ever. "Well, you're not in charge," he told Lucille in a furious voice. "In fact, as of right now, you don't even work here anymore!"

Wow! Lucille had been fired! Now Katie felt really guilty. The food fight wasn't Lucille's fault. Katie wished she could run into Mr. Kane's office and tell him that it was her fault, but she knew the principal wouldn't believe her. A girl who turned into a lunch lady when a magical wind blew on her? Katie shook her head. Nobody would ever believe a story like that.

Quickly, Katie hurried back to the cafeteria. The least she could do was help the other kids clean up.

Chapter 6

That afternoon, Katie sat in her room with the door closed. She didn't feel very much like going out to play. Even if she did feel like playing, there'd be no one to play with. Most of the kids from school were grounded because they'd been in the food fight.

Still, Katie bet that none of the other kids felt as bad as she did. All they had lost was an afternoon of TV or a trip to the playground. Katie had made Lucille lose her job.

Katie began to cry. As soon as he saw Katie's tears, Pepper jumped up on the bed and sat beside her. He stuck out his big, red tongue and licked her face. But even a big,

sloppy, wet, dog-kiss couldn't cheer up Katie.
She used the back of her hand to wipe
Pepper's slobber from her cheek. Pepper lifted
his back paw and scratched at his floppy ear.

Just then there was a knock at the door.
"Katie, Suzanne is on the phone," her mother
said.

Katie walked downstairs to the kitchen
and picked up the phone. "Hi, Suzanne," she
said.

"Hey," Suzanne answered. "Where were
you during the food fight today?"

"I . . . um . . . er . . . I was in the bathroom,"
Katie stammered. She hated lying to her
friend, but she just couldn't tell her what had
really happened.

"I can't believe you missed the whole
thing," Suzanne continued. "It was amazing.
Food was flying all over the place. I don't
think I'll ever get the tomato juice off of my
sweater. Kevin hit me in the back with a really
squishy one!"

"Did it hurt?" Katie asked her.

"Nah," Suzanne said. "It was too mushy to hurt. It just sort of slid down my back. Besides, I got Kevin back—big time! I poured a container of grape juice over his head! His whole face turned purple. He looked like a space alien."

Katie giggled, a little.

"I don't think it's fair that Mrs. Derkman made you clean up with everyone else. You weren't even there." Suzanne continued. "It's such a bummer that you were in the bathroom! Katie, you always miss the good stuff."

"I heard all about it, though," Katie told Suzanne. "The whole school was talking about it when I got back to the cafeteria."

"But I'll bet you don't know what happened *after* the food fight," Suzanne said.

Katie smiled. Suzanne loved knowing things before anybody else did.

"What?" Katie asked her.

"Guess," Suzanne answered.

"Come on, Suzanne. Just tell me," Katie urged.

"Lucille the lunch lady got fired!" Suzanne exclaimed. "Mr. Kane told my mom when she came to pick me up. He said that he couldn't let a lunch lady who acted like an eight-year-old work in the school."

Katie felt guilty all over again.

"The weird thing was, Lucille *was* kinda acting like a kid," Suzanne continued. "I heard she told Malcolm the food belonged in the garbage. She even threw a bunch of it."

"That wasn't any reason to fire her," Katie interrupted her. "The food *is* really gross. We should have healthier stuff to eat."

"I guess," Suzanne agreed.

"And you know what else?" Katie continued. "Lucille didn't even really start the food fight. She was throwing some food out in the garbage and it landed on George by mistake. He started the food fight."

"How do you know that?" Suzanne asked her suddenly. "You weren't even there."

Oops! Katie had forgotten that she was supposed to have been in the girls' room during the food fight. "Well, that's what I heard, anyway," she lied. "A bunch of kids said George was the one who yelled out 'food fight!' Maybe Mr. Kane should have fired him instead."

Suzanne laughed. "Mr. Kane can't fire a kid," she told Katie. "Kids have to go to school. It's a law."

"Well, anyway, it wasn't fair of Mr. Kane to fire Lucille," Katie continued.

"Oh who cares?" Suzanne said. "She's just a grouchy lunch lady. Besides, it was her own fault."

"She made a mistake," Katie insisted. "How'd you like it if you got punished every time you made a mistake? Everyone deserves a second chance—even grouches."

"I guess," Suzanne finally agreed. "But what can we do about it? We're just kids."

Katie was quiet for a minute, thinking. Suddenly an idea exploded in her head. "Suzanne, do you think you can bring a bag lunch for school tomorrow?" she asked excitedly.

"Sure, I guess so," Suzanne answered.

"Good. So will I," Katie said. "We have to call everyone we know and ask them to pack their lunches, too. Let's make sure every kid in the whole school brings a bag lunch tomorrow."

"I don't get it," Suzanne admitted. "How is that going to get Lucille her job back?"

"Nobody in our school is going to buy a cafeteria lunch until Lucille is back behind the counter!" Katie explained. "We're on a cafeteria strike!"

As soon as she hung up the phone with Suzanne, Katie called Jeremy and told him about the cafeteria strike. He had to let the boys know not to bring lunch money tomorrow.

"I don't know, Katie. Are you sure the kids will want to help Lucille?" Jeremy asked after Katie explained the plan to him. "She *is* kind of mean."

"Well, we're not so nice to her, either. All we ever do is complain about the food," Katie told him. "And she has a really hard job. It's hot back there in the kitchen. And she's standing up all the time. You wouldn't believe how badly her feet hurt!"

"How do you know that?" Jeremy asked.

Katie gulped. She'd almost let Jeremy know what had happened to her today. She needed to be more careful about what she said. "I . . . um . . . I'm just guessing that's how she feels," she stammered nervously. "Anyway, maybe Lucille would like us better if she knew we'd tried to get her job back for her."

"Maybe," Jeremy agreed. "She probably wouldn't have gotten fired if the food fight hadn't gotten wild. I guess it's kind of partly our fault."

"Exactly," Katie said. "That's why we should do this for her."

"It's worth a try, anyhow," Jeremy agreed. "What do you want me to do?"

"Just call two or three boys in our class and tell them about the strike," Katie instructed him. "Ask them to call a few of their friends. Then those kids can tell more kids, and they can tell more kids. If we keep the chain going all afternoon, by tomorrow everyone will know about the strike."

"I'll try," Jeremy assured Katie. "I hope it works."

"This plan has got to work," Katie answered. "It just has to!"

Chapter 7

The next morning, Katie had a lot of trouble sitting still in class. All she could think about was the cafeteria strike. Katie wasn't sure if all the kids in school had gotten phone calls. She wondered if everyone had agreed to bring their own lunches. If even one kid decided to buy lunch, the plan wouldn't work. They all had to stick together.

Luckily, as soon as she walked into the cafeteria, Katie knew she had nothing to worry about. No one was buying the school lunch. The cafeteria tables were covered with brown bags and lunch boxes the kids had brought from home.

Katie looked toward the counter. There was a new lunch lady standing there. She was short and chubby, with small gray eyes and big, yellow teeth. She looked *really* mean. She also looked really bored. None of the kids were buying lunch. The new lunch lady had nothing to do.

Katie smiled happily as she opened up her lunch bag.

"I thought you said your mom didn't have time to make you lunch in the morning," Suzanne remarked.

"She doesn't," Katie answered. "I made this myself." She took a big bite of her peanut butter and jelly sandwich. "It's pretty good. What do you have?"

Suzanne pulled a small plastic container from her brown bag. Inside the container were six evenly cut pieces of sushi. Suzanne took a pair of chopsticks from the bag and began to eat.

Katie glanced over at the next table where

the boys were sitting. Ever since Suzanne and Jeremy had argued over Speedy, the boys and girls in class 3A sat at separate tables. Katie felt bad about not being able to sit near Jeremy at lunch.

Of all the lunches in the cafeteria, George's was the most amazing. Most of the kids had brought lunch boxes or little brown bags with them to school. But not George. He was carrying a huge brown bag, the kind you got when you brought groceries home from the supermarket. Slowly, he began to empty the bag. First he unpacked a huge hero sandwich. Then he took out a pickle and a container of potato salad. Next he opened his Thermos and poured himself a cup of juice. Finally, he pulled a bag of corn chips out of the bag.

"Wow! That's some lunch!" Kevin exclaimed loud enough for Katie and the other girls to hear. "George, you are such a pig!"

George bit off a huge hunk of his hero and

began to snort. "Look at me, I'm a pig!" he shouted as he snorted.

"He's not kidding!" Suzanne said. "Only a pig would talk with his mouth full."

George leaned over toward the girls' table. He opened his mouth wide so Suzanne and Katie could see his half-chewed sandwich. "Hey, Katie Kazoo, check this out. I have seafood for lunch!" he told her. "Get it? *See* food?"

Katie giggled. George was definitely gross. He was also pretty funny.

"Speaking of pigs," George began as he swallowed his food. "What do you get when you mix a pig and an egg?"

"I don't know," Jeremy answered him. "What?"

"*Ham*pty Dumpty!" George exclaimed.

"Good one, George." Jeremy laughed. "I love your jokes."

"I've got a million of 'em!" George assured him. "What rescued Hampty Dumpty when he fell off the wall?"

"What?" Kevin asked.

"A *ham*bulance, of course," George replied. He chuckled really hard at his own joke.

Katie turned toward the food counter. The new lunch lady was still standing there. Her face looked a little sweaty now—probably because there was a lot of steam coming up from the food trays.

Just then, Mr. Kane walked into the cafeteria. The principal looked around the room. He stared at all the lunch boxes and brown

paper bags on the tables. Then he headed
toward the lunch line. Katie watched as Mr.
Kane stared at all the uneaten food.

"What's going on in here?" Mr. Kane asked
the new lunch lady.

"I don't know," she answered him.
"Nobody's buying lunch."

Mr. Kane nodded his head slowly. Then he
turned and faced the kids.

"Okay, kids, what's going on in here? Why
isn't anyone buying lunch?" the principal asked.

" 'Cause we're on strike," a boy from the
kindergarten called out. The grown-up words

sounded funny coming from such a little boy. Everyone started to laugh, even Mr. Kane.

"You are?" Mr. Kane kneeled down next to him. "Why, Joshua?"

" 'Cause the lunch lady went away. We want her back," Josh explained.

Katie smiled as she watched the principal stand up and look around at all the brown bags and lunch boxes in the cafeteria. Now that he understood why the kids weren't buying lunches, Katie was sure the principal was going to tell them that Lucille could have her job back.

Katie sat up straight. She was about to be a hero.

But Katie was wrong. Mr. Kane didn't say a word. He just walked out of the room. Katie slumped down in her seat. This was not going to be as easy as she'd thought.

The students of Cherrydale Elementary School were not quitters. The next day they all brought their own lunches to school again. Once more, the new lunch lady stood all alone behind her trays. She looked even more angry, bored, and sweaty than she had the day before.

Katie took her seat next to Suzanne at the girls' table and opened her lunch bag.

"What do you have today?" Suzanne asked her.

"Peanut butter and jelly," Katie answered.

"Again?" Suzanne said.

Katie shrugged. "It's the only thing I know how to make. What have you got?"

"My mother gave me some leftover pizza with extra cheese," Suzanne said. "I like to eat it cold."

Katie glanced over toward the boys' table. Jeremy had brought a big bag of jelly beans to school. He was busy sharing them with Kevin and Carlos. Katie knew that if she were sitting over there, Jeremy would have let her have some of the purple ones. But the other boys didn't want Katie—or any of the girls—sitting at their table.

Katie sure wished that Jeremy and Suzanne would stop fighting over the hamster. Their fight was ruining the whole class. Besides, they had to decide something fast. Tomorrow was Friday. Speedy still didn't have a home to go to for the weekend!

Katie also hoped that Mr. Kane would decide to hire Lucille back soon. The cafeteria was really starting to smell because of the strike. Since no one had bought the hot dogs yesterday, the lunch lady had brought them out again. School hot dogs always smelled pretty bad, but *day-old* school hot dogs really stank.

Just then, Mr. Kane walked toward the front of the cafeteria and looked out at the students. "It looks like we have a lot of uneaten food today, just like yesterday," he told them in a loud, stern voice. "I suppose it will be the same way tomorrow, too," he added.

Katie gulped. Mr. Kane sounded a little bit angry about the cafeteria strike. She was also pretty sure he was looking in her direction when he spoke. Did Mr. Kane know that Katie had started the cafeteria strike? Was he going to be angry with her? For the first time, Katie was worried about how the cafeteria strike was going to turn out.

But just then, Mr. Kane's stern frown turned upside down. He smiled at the children. "Well, I have good news for you kids," the principal said. "Lucille and I spoke on the phone today. I told her I thought she deserved a second chance."

Katie smiled. That's what she thought, too.

"You'll all be glad to know that Lucille said she'd come back to work . . . if you all promised to be good at lunch time," Mr. Kane told them.

"Hooray!" The kids in the cafeteria cheered.

"She also made me promise that we would have some better-tasting food and fresher vegetables. Starting tomorrow, we will have a different menu in the cafeteria."

"Hooray!" Once again, the kids began to shout wildly.

Mr. Kane looked sternly at the cheering kids. Everyone got quiet really quickly. "But

your food fight made a big mess of this room. We'll never get these walls completely cleaned up. You kids will have to stay after school for a few days to paint them."

Now the kids looked really sad. Painting the walls sounded like a boring job.

Just then, Katie had an idea. She raised her hand shyly. Mr. Kane looked over at her. "Yes, Katie," he said.

"Do we have to paint the walls this same color? Or can we paint a big picture on the wall instead?" she asked.

Mr. Kane thought about that for a minute. Then he nodded. "That's a wonderful idea, Katie. It would be nice to have a mural that was painted by our students." He smiled at the kids. "This cafeteria strike has proven that you can do great things when you all work together. I can't wait to see what kind of painting you can come up with."

"This is going to be the most beautiful cafeteria ever!" Katie assured the principal.

Chapter 8

The kids in class 3A began planning the mural as soon as Mr. Kane left the cafeteria.

"I think we should have unicorns and stars," Suzanne suggested.

"Oh yeah," Zoe agreed. "That sounds so pretty."

Kevin sat at the boys' table and rolled his eyes. "Would you listen to those girls? Who wants a *pretty* mural? I say we go for cool stuff like skateboards and hot-air balloons."

"Sounds good to me," Jeremy agreed.

"I'm not painting any dumb unicorn," George said.

That did it. Katie got up and stood right

between the two tables.

"Cut it out!" she shouted. "I'm tired of everybody fighting."

"It's her fault," Jeremy said, pointing at Suzanne.

"Are you nuts?" Suzanne shouted. "You started it."

"I don't care who started it," Katie said. "If we keep fighting we won't have any mural at all. We all have to work together."

"Okay, so what's it gonna be, Katie Kazoo? Skateboarders or unicorns?" George asked.

"I don't know," Katie admitted. "Maybe we could come up with something else. Something we're all happy with."

The kids thought about that for a minute.

"Okay," Suzanne agreed.

"You're right, Katie," Jeremy said quietly.

"So we're all friends again?" Katie asked nervously.

"I guess," Jeremy said. He looked across the aisle at Suzanne. "If we keep fighting over

Speedy, he won't have any place to go this weekend. Why don't you take him?"

Katie was surprised. She knew how badly Jeremy had wanted to take Speedy to his house.

Katie was even *more* surprised by Suzanne's answer.

"No, he's better off with you," Suzanne said. "Heather's stuff is pretty much all over my whole house. Everywhere you look there's a stroller or a changing table or a crib. I don't think there'd be any room for a hamster playground."

"But you know I have that big game on Saturday. I'm going to be busy with that," Jeremy told her.

Katie was worried all over again. Now it didn't sound like *either* of her friends wanted to take Speedy home. She had to do something fast!

"I have an idea," Katie said quickly. "Jeremy, you keep Speedy at your place.

Suzanne can come over on Saturday morning to give him his food and water while you're at the game."

"That's a good idea," Suzanne agreed. "Hey, and maybe on Sunday we could build him a hamster playground . . . together."

"Cool!" Jeremy exclaimed. "You know, my dad has a huge shoe box. It could be a cave."

"I'll bring over some paper towel rolls for Speedy to climb through," Suzanne said.

Katie sat quietly as she listened to Jeremy  and Suzanne's plans for the hamster playground. She was really happy that her two best friends were getting along so well. She was also kind of sad. They were leaving her out of everything!

Jeremy guessed how Katie was feeling.

"Can you come over and help us build the playground?" he asked her.

Now Katie smiled brightly. "You bet!" she exclaimed.

Lunchtime was a whole lot more fun the next day. Katie stood on the lunch line right between her two best friends. It was nice not to have to choose between them any more.

When she reached the front of the line, Katie smiled brightly at Lucille. "I'll have a veggie wimpy and a cow juice," she told the lunch Lady. "And for dessert I'd like an Eve with a lid."

Lucille looked at Katie with surprise. She had no idea where the third-grader had learned the secret lunchroom language, but she gave Katie a veggie burger, a container of milk, and a slice of apple pie anyway.

"Thanks," Katie told her. "It's good to have you back."

Lucille didn't say anything, but Katie thought she saw her smile a little.

As Katie followed Jeremy to a table near the back of the cafeteria, she felt a slight breeze blowing on the back of her neck. Katie looked around nervously. Was she about to change into someone else . . . right here in front of the whole school?

As Katie looked around, she noticed that the door to the playground was wide open. This was no magic wind. It was just a normal, everyday, outside kind of wind. Katie wasn't changing into anyone. She was staying Katie Kazoo.

At least for now.

Yummy Lunch Recipies!

Do you find the same old peanut-butter-and-jelly sandwiches in your lunch box every day? Are you sick of hard-boiled eggs and tuna salad? Well, here's the cure to the boring food blues. These easy-to-make lunch recipes are favorites of the kids in room 3A. Try them all. They're guaranteed to tickle your taste buds!

And after you've filled the inside of your lunch bag with these tasty treats, don't forget about the outside of the bag. Decorate your paper bag with stickers or funny pictures, just to make lunch time more special!

Cracker Stacker

You will need: round crackers, peanut butter, grape jelly.

Here's what you do: Start with a plain cracker. Spread  peanut butter on the cracker. Put a second cracker on top of the first. Spread jelly on the second cracker. Put a third cracker on top of the second cracker. Spread peanut butter on that one. Then top that cracker with a fourth cracker. Spread jelly on the top cracker. Keep going until you have a stack of crackers. Wrap your cracker stack in waxed paper before putting it in your lunch box.

Banana Dogs

You will need: one banana, a hot dog roll, peanut butter.

Here's what you do: Place the banana in the hot dog roll. Smear the banana with peanut butter just the way you would smear mustard on a hot dog. Wrap up your banana dog in waxed paper and pack it in your lunch bag.

Inside-Out Sandwiches

You will need: one slice of bologna (use soy bologna slices if you're a vegetarian like Katie), one slice of American cheese, cream cheese, peanut butter, two bread sticks.

Here's what you do: Lay out the slices of
bologna and cheese. Spread cream
cheese on one side of the balogna.
Spread peanut butter on one
side of the American cheese
slice. Take one bread stick and
wrap the meat around it. Make sure the
cream cheese side is touching the bread stick.
Wrap the American cheese slice around the
second bread stick. Make sure the peanut butter side is touching the bread stick. Now you
have two inside-out sandwiches. (The bread
[stick]) is in the middle. Get it?) Place the sandwiches in a sealed sandwich bag and pack them
in your lunch bag.

Shape-up Sandwiches

You will need: cream cheese,
two slices of white or whole-wheat bread,
raisins, grape jelly, cookie cutters.

Here's what you do: Spread cream cheese

on one slice of bread. Sprinkle raisins on top of the cream cheese. Spread grape jelly on the other slice of bread. Place that slice on top of the raisins and cream cheese with the jelly-side-down. Use the cookie cutters to cut your sandwich into different shapes. Place your shaped sandwiches into plastic bags to keep them fresh.

A Gobble Gobble Good Sandwich

You will need: mayonnaise, three slices of white or whole wheat bread, two slices of turkey (or soy turkey), cran-berry sauce, leftover stuffing.

Here's what you do: Spread a thin layer of mayonnaise on one slice of bread. Top the mayonnaise with turkey slices. Add the next slice of bread. Spread cranberry sauce on top of the bread. Place the stuffing on top of the cranberry sauce. Top with the last piece of bread. Store the sandwich in a plastic bag.